Farmyard Tales Flip Books
The Grumpy Goat

Heather Amery

Illustrated by Stephen Cartwright

Language consultant: Betty Root
Series editor: Jenny Tyler

There is a little yellow duck to find on every page.

This is Apple Tree Farm.

This is Mrs. Boot, the farmer. She has two children, called Poppy and Sam, and a dog called Rusty.

Ted works on the farm.

He tells Poppy and Sam to clean the goat's shed.
"Will she let us?" asks Sam. "She's so grumpy now."

Gertie the goat chases Sam.

She butts him with her head. He nearly falls over.
Sam, Poppy and Rusty run out through the gate.

Poppy shuts the gate.

They must get Gertie out of her pen so they can
get to her shed. "I have an idea," says Sam.

Sam gets a bag of bread.

"Come on, Gertie," says Sam. "Nice bread."
Gertie eats it and the bag, but stays in her pen.

"Let's try some fresh grass," says Poppy.

Poppy pulls up some grass and drops it by the gate.
Gertie eats it but trots back into her pen.

"I have another idea," says Sam.

"Gertie doesn't butt Ted. She wouldn't butt me if
I looked like Ted," says Sam. He runs off again.

Sam comes back wearing Ted's clothes.

He has found Ted's old coat and hat. Sam goes
into the pen but Gertie still butts him.

"I'll get a rope," says Poppy.

They go into the pen. Poppy tries to throw the rope over Gertie's head. She misses.

Gertie chases them all.

Rusty runs out of the pen and Gertie follows him.
"She's out!" shouts Sam. "Quick, shut the gate."

Sam and Poppy clean out Gertie's shed.

They sweep up the old straw and put it in the
wheelbarrow. They spread out fresh straw.

Poppy opens the gate.

"Come on, Gertie. You can go back now," says Sam.
Gertie trots back into her pen.

"You are a grumpy old goat," says Poppy.

"We've cleaned out your shed and you're still grumpy," says Sam. "Grumpy Gertie."

Next morning, they meet Ted.

"Come and look at Gertie now," says Ted. They all
go to the goat pen.

Gertie has a little kid.

"Oh, isn't it sweet," says Poppy. "Gertie doesn't look grumpy now," says Sam.

"Let's all go home now," says Mrs. Boot.

They take the sheep back to the farm. "I think Woolly just wanted a ride on the train," says Sam.

"How many passengers?" says the guard.

"Six sheep, one dog and four people," says Mrs. Boot.
"That's all."

The train puffs along.

It stops at the station. Mrs. Boot opens the door.
Poppy and Sam jump down onto the platform.

"All aboard!"

Poppy, Sam, Mrs. Boot, Ted and Rusty climb up
into the carriage. Mrs. Boot waves to the driver.

"We'll lift them up."

"Please help me, Ted," says Mrs. Boot. Ted and
Mrs. Boot lift the sheep up into the carriage.

"Come on, Woolly."

They drive the sheep down the track to the train.
Woolly runs away but Rusty chases her back.

"How can we get them home?"

"We can't get them up the bank," says Ted.
"We'll put them on the train," says Mrs. Boot.

"We must move them."

"You can help me," says Mrs. Boot. "Come on,
Rusty," says Sam. They walk up to the sheep.

"It's that naughty Woolly."

"She's escaped from her field again," says Poppy.
"She wanted to see the steam train," says Sam.

"Look at those sheep."

"They are on the track," says Poppy. "That's why the train has stopped." "Silly sheep," says Sam.

Soon they come to the train track.

They can just see the old steam train. It has stopped but is still puffing and whistling.

"We'll go and look."

"Poppy and Sam can come too," says Mrs. Boot.
"And Rusty," says Sam. They walk across the fields.

"What's the matter, Ted?" asks Mrs. Boot.

"The train is in trouble. I think it's stuck. I can hear it whistling and whistling," says Ted.

This is Ted.

He drives the tractor and helps Mrs. Boot on the farm. He waves and shouts to Mrs. Boot.